TOP
HIGH SCHOOL SPORTS

VOLLEYBALL

A Crabtree Branches Book

THOMAS KINGSLEY TROUPE

CRABTREE
Publishing Company
www.crabtreebooks.com

School-to-Home Support for Caregivers and Teachers

This high-interest book is designed to motivate striving students with engaging topics while building fluency, vocabulary, and an interest in reading. Here are a few questions and activities to help the reader build upon his or her comprehension skills.

Before Reading:

- *What do I think this book is about?*
- *What do I know about this topic?*
- *What do I want to learn about this topic?*
- *Why am I reading this book?*

During Reading:

- *I wonder why...*
- *I'm curious to know...*
- *How is this like something I already know?*
- *What have I learned so far?*

After Reading:

- *What was the author trying to teach me?*
- *What are some details?*
- *How did the photographs and captions help me understand more?*
- *Read the book again and look for the vocabulary words.*
- *What questions do I still have?*

Extension Activities:

- *What was your favorite part of the book? Write a paragraph on it.*
- *Draw a picture of your favorite thing you learned from the book.*

TABLE OF CONTENTS

SPIKE IT!

You toss the volleyball up and smash your serve over the net. The **libero** on the other team passes it up to the setter. Their hitter drives the ball back across the net, whistling between your teammates. You dive and bump the ball to your teammate who spikes it and scores!

Strap on your gym shoes and practice your **vertical**! We're about to learn why volleyball ranks among the... TOP HIGH SCHOOL SPORTS.

VOLLEYBALL HISTORY

William G. Morgan

The sport of volleyball was created in Massachusetts by a YMCA instructor named William G. Morgan in 1895. Back then it was called Mintonette.

Volleyball borrows from a number of different sports, including basketball, tennis, and handball. Morgan wanted to create a sport for businessmen that had less physical contact than basketball.

During a demonstration of the game, someone noticed the players were volleying the ball back and forth. It was decided volleyball would be a better name for the sport.

VOLLEYBALL SEASON

For many high schools, volleyball season for girls starts in late August or early September and continues to the end of October. For schools that have boys' teams, volleyball is a spring sport from March until May.

Volleyball was typically a girls sport, but more and more state high schools have started teams for boys, too!

FUN FACT

The first game of volleyball was played on July 7, 1896, at Springfield College in Springfield, Massachusetts.

HIGH SCHOOL VOLLEYBALL TEAMS

Most high schools have four volleyball teams, depending on player interest and school size. The two varsity teams are often third- or fourth-year students. More experienced volleyball players play on the varsity teams.

The other two teams are junior varsity teams. Junior varsity teams are where first- and second-year students build their skills. Players who do well on the JV team will move to the varsity team in third or fourth year.

Volleyball became a medal sport in 1964 at the Tokyo Olympics. The sport featured two events: a tournament for women and a separate competition for men. In 1996, beach volleyball was added as an Olympic sport for both women and men.

BASICS OF THE GAME

Volleyball is a fairly simple sport to learn. There are six players on each team. Three play on the front row and three play on the back row. The ball is served from the back row and must make it across the net.

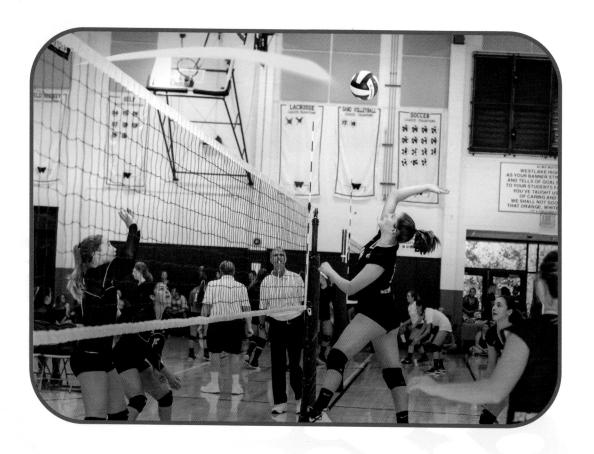

Players have three hits to get it back across the net. If the ball doesn't get back over the net or it goes out of bounds, the other team receives the point. Matches are usually three to five sets where the first team to 25 points wins, but must win by two points.

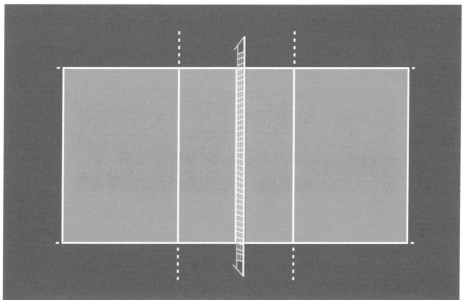

VOLLEYBALL POSITIONS

Setter — This player runs the team's **offense**, much like a quarterback in football. The setter usually touches the ball second, setting it up for the attacking player.

Outside Hitter —
(Left-Side Hitter) This player attacks from the left and should have good jumping ability. This position is the go-to on offense and completes most attack hits.

Outside Hitter —
(Right-Side Hitter) This player attacks from the right and is good at both offense and **defense**. They should have good jumping skills too. This player should be ready to set if the setter can't get to the ball.

OUTSIDE HITTER

High school volleyball uses what is called the rally system. This means that regardless of who serves the ball, the team who keeps the ball in play wins the point. The old system of side-out scoring was phased out, although some schools may still use it. With side out, only the serving team could score. The receiving side would try to win the volley to get a chance to serve and score.

Middle Blocker (Hitter) — This position is usually filled by the team's tallest player. The middle blocker can block shots coming across the center of the net. The hitter will also use quick attacks on offense.

Libero — This position truly focuses on defense. The libero only plays in the back row and usually receives a serve or an attack. A libero needs to be good at passing, too. This player often wears a different colored jersey.

Defensive Specialist — This player replaces another in the back row who might not be as strong defensively. While a libero can only play the back row, a defensive specialist can play in the front row if needed.

LIBERO

DEFENSIVE SPECIALIST

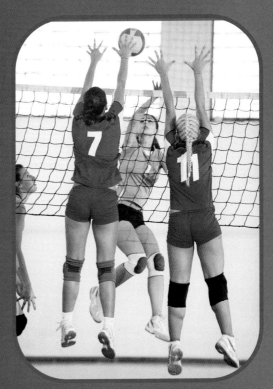

MIDDLE BLOCKER

BASIC MOVES

Forearm Passing (Bumping) — when a player uses their forearms to redirect or pass the ball to a teammate

Volleying — use of fingertips to knock the ball back over the net

Setting — pushing the ball up to set the ball up for a teammate to smash it over the net

Attacking — using a one-armed overhead swing to strike the ball with an open hand. If done with power, it can slam the ball into opponent **territory**

Diving — leaping to hit a low ball and prevent it from touching the floor

Blocking — jumping at the net with arms up to block the opponent's ball from coming across the net

Serving — using an **underhand** or **overhand** hit to send the ball over the net to begin a new play

SETTING

VOLLEYING

DIVING

SERVING

High school volleyball teams have six players on the court at once. Beach volleyball is played with a team of two against two. They have two positions: blocker and defender, and a volleyball match is played to 21 points instead of 25.

EQUIPMENT AND UNIFORMS

High school volleyball is a competitive sport where a lot of action takes place. Players will need good gym shoes, a pair of knee and elbow pads, and a mouth guard to protect their teeth.

FUN FACT

Most volleyball players jump around 300 times per match. That's quite the workout!

Volleyball players wear shorts and a short sleeve or tank-top jersey. Most schools will have their school's name, mascot, and player's number and last name on the back.

PRACTICE AND TRAINING

A lot of high schools will start volleyball practice a month or so before the school year starts. Regular practices are held after school in the gymnasium and will last for an hour or an hour and a half.

Players can expect to work on basic skills, setting up plays, **agility**, and stamina drills.

VOLLEYBALL JARGON

Like most sports, volleyball uses odd names and phrases that might confuse new players at first!

Here are some to get you started:

Ace — a serve that lands on the opponent's side without any players touching it and is a instant point

Dig — a defensive save from an opponent's attack

Kill — a legal, point-scoring spike attack

Lift — when a ball is carried with an open hand or the player touches it too long before bumping or passing. Referees will call this and a point will be given to the other team

Shank — a bad, unplayable pass to another player

Team Side Switch — teams switch sides of the net every seven cumulative points

Three Touches — meaning the ball can only be touched by players on one side three times before it's sent over the net

PLAYOFFS AND STATE TOURNAMENTS

High school volleyball teams work hard all season to come out on top. If they do well, they can compete in state playoffs and state championship **tournaments**.

Like other sports, teams are broken in classes, based on the number of students enrolled in the high school. This makes for fair competition where smaller schools will play against smaller schools and bigger schools face off against big schools.

FUN FACT

The longest volleyball game on record was played in Kingston, North Carolina. It lasted for 75 hours and 30 minutes. This was due to the old side-out scoring system!

CONCLUSION

Volleyball is one of the most exciting and challenging sports high-schoolers can play. It takes teamwork, skill, and **precision** to win the game. Volleyball fans love to watch a good match!

Will you step up to the net and spike the ball to victory? Maybe you and your team will end up competing with the best teams. With practice and a great serve, you'll see why volleyball is easily one of the TOP HIGH SCHOOL SPORTS!

GLOSSARY

agility (uh-JIL-uh-tee): to move quickly and easily

defense (DEE-fenss): defending against the opposing team's attacks at the net

libero (LEE-buh-roh): rearmost defensive player in volleyball

offense (AW-fenss): the team possessing the ball in an attempt to score

overhand (AW-fenss): with the palm downward or inward

precision (pri-SIZH-uhn): exact or accurate

territory (TER-uh-tor-ee): an area defended by a team or play in a game or sport

tournaments (TOR-nuh-muhntz): a series of contests or games played between competing teams

underhand (UHN-dur-hand): with the palm upward or outward

vertical (VUR-ti-kuhl): the highest point of a high jump in volleyball

INDEX

WEBSITES TO VISIT

https://kids.kiddle.co/Volleyball

https://kids.lovetoknow.com/kids-activities/
volleyball-games-kids

https://www.ducksters.com/sports/volleyball.php

ABOUT THE AUTHOR

Thomas Kingsley Troupe

Thomas Kingsley Troupe is the author of a big ol' pile of books for kids. He's written about everything from ghosts to Bigfoot to third grade werewolves. He even wrote a book about dirt. When he's not writing or reading, he gets plenty of exercise and remembers sacking quarterbacks while on his high school football team. Thomas lives in Woodbury, Minnesota with his two sons.

CRABTREE
Publishing Company

Written by: Thomas Kingsley Troupe
Designed by: Jennifer Dydyk
Edited by: Kelli Hicks
Proofreader: Ellen Rodger

Photographs: Following images from Shutterstock.com: Cover background pattern (and pattern throughout book) © HNK, volleyball on cover and title page © Praneat, cover photo of male players © Monkey Business Images, cover photo of female players © ESB Professional. Page 7 © Max4e Photo, Pages 9, 10 © Monkey Business Images, Page 13 (bottom photo) © softpixel, Page 14 player duplicated on court © f_y_b, Page 15 (top photo) © dotshock, (bottom photo) © Monkey Business Images, Page 16 © HDmytro, Page 17 (top) © Monkey Business Images, (middle blocker) © ESB Professional, Page 19 all photos © Master1305, Page 21 ball © gresei, players © Artur Didyk, Page 22 © Paolo Bona, Page 23 top photo © Monkey Business Images, bottom photo © Master1305, Page 24 bottom photo © muzsy, Page 25 © Trong Nguyen, Page 27 © Iurii Sivokon, Page 29 top photo © Monkey Business Images, bottom photo © f_y_b. Following images from istock by Getty Images: Pages 4 and 5 © Artur Didyk. Following images from Dreamstime.com: Page 5 ball © Tetiana Miroshnichenko, Pages 8, 11, 13 (top photo), © Sports Images, Page 12 © Jon Osumi, Page 14 illustration of court © Lesik Aleksandr, Page 17 (defensive specialist) © Sports Images, Page 20 © Cosmin Iftode, Page 24 top photo and Page 26 © Jon Osumi, Page 28 © Sports Images. Page 6 public domain image from Official Volley Ball Rules, 1916-1917.

Library and Archives Canada
Cataloguing in Publication

CIP available at Library and
Archives Canada

Library of Congress Cataloging-in-Publication Data

CIP available at Library of Congress

Crabtree Publishing Company   Printed in the U.S.A./CG20210915/012022

www.crabtreebooks.com   1-800-387-7650

Published in the United States
Crabtree Publishing
347 Fifth Avenue, Suite 1402-145
New York, NY, 10016

Published in Canada
Crabtree Publishing
616 Welland Ave.
St. Catharines, Ontario L2M 5V6